The Jumping Alien!

Story by Michael Pryor
Illustrations by Forrest Burdett

Contents

Chapter 1

Finding Zorgbon

Sanjay walked up and down near the sports ground at school. Where was Zorgbon? He was going to be late for the high-jump competition!

A teacher saw Sanjay and came over. “You look worried, Sanjay. Is anything wrong?”

Sanjay sighed. “Zorgbon’s not here, Ms Edo. I’ve tried his phone but he’s not answering.”

"You've been coaching Zorgbon in the high jump, haven't you?" asked Ms Edo.

"Yes, for months," replied Sanjay. "He's really good, but he doesn't think he is."

"He has long legs," said Ms Edo. "He looks like he would be a good high jumper."

"Zorgbon's the best," said Sanjay. "He can jump as high as anything."

"He could be sick, I suppose," said Ms Edo.

"Maybe. I think he's just scared of failing," said Sanjay.

Ms Edo looked at her watch. "Do you know where Zorgbon lives?"

"Yes. It's not far," Sanjay said. "I can go and get him. I promise we'll come straight back."

"You're a good friend, Sanjay."

The bus stopped right outside Zorgbon's house. Sanjay jumped off the bus, ran up the stairs and banged on the front door.

"I know you're in there, Zorgbon! Hurry up or we'll be late!"

Zorgbon opened the door. He was taller than Sanjay and his skin was bright blue. He had a nose like an elephant's trunk, long, skinny legs and big, sad eyes.

"Hello, Sanjay," he said. "I don't feel so good."

"Do you want to feel better?" Sanjay asked.

Zorgbon scratched his head. "I think so."

"Then imagine how good you'll feel when you win the high-jump competition!" Sanjay said, hopping from one foot to the other with excitement.

Zorgbon groaned. “I can’t, Sanjay. I’m hopeless. I’ll trip over. I’ll bang the bar with my head. I’ll miss the landing bags. Everyone will laugh at me.”

Sanjay grabbed Zorgbon's long, skinny arm. "You're the best high jumper in the school, Zorgbon – better than all of the other students. *I* know that, even if you don't."

"Really?" Zorgbon said.

"Trust me," Sanjay said. "We have to go now. We don't have a moment to lose."

Chapter 2

The Alien Day Parade

On the bus, Zorgbon rubbed his hands together nervously. "Is there any wind at the sports ground?" he asked Sanjay. "I don't like wind. It ruins my run-up."

"No wind," Sanjay said. "It's a perfect day for high jumping."

Sanjay peered past the bus driver. There were lots of cars on the road. What would they do if there was a traffic jam?

The bus stopped with a sudden jolt.
"Everyone has to get off," the driver said.

Sanjay stood up. "What's wrong?" he asked the driver.

"Nothing's wrong," the driver said. She pointed ahead. "It's the big Alien Day Parade. All the roads are blocked until lunchtime."

Sanjay slapped his forehead. He'd forgotten about the Alien Day Parade! Once a year, all the happy aliens living in the city would march to the town hall.

The Fleenbeens, like Zorgbon, would play their musical instruments. The Hoffians would use all eight of their arms to juggle clubs, plates and balls. The giant Vespians would carry children on their backs while blowing multi-coloured bubbles from their snouts. The round Snerdians would leapfrog down the street as fast as lightning. The Orpians would hand out their famous holographic ice cream – everyone's favourite!

And the crowd would clog the streets for hours.

Zorgbon shook his head as he and Sanjay got off the bus.
"We'll *never* get to the sports ground in time.
I knew I should have stayed in bed."

Chapter 3

Disaster at the Parade!

The streets were full of people.

The aliens in the parade were colourful, musical and spectacular. The Hoffians threw their juggling clubs, plates and balls high in the air and caught them. The Fleenbeens played their pipes, thumped their drums and plucked their strings. The Vespians blew bubbles and made the children on their backs laugh. The Snerdians bounced along while singing in their deep voices. The Orpians handed out holographic ice creams.

They all waved, and the people cheered.

ALIEN DAY PARADE

Sanjay and Zorgbon were the only ones who weren't happy.

Sanjay shook his head. This wasn't a parade – it was a disaster! It would take them hours to get back to the sports ground!

The giant Vespians marched past, each one as big as a bus. Sanjay liked all aliens, but especially Vespians. He thought they looked like stripy triceratops, because they snapped their beaks when they were happy.

When they marched, their four enormous feet made the ground shake. The lucky children riding on their backs waved red, green and purple flags.

A young Vespian was at the back of the Vespian group. He was only as big as a car and he was smiling broadly.

"I have an idea," Sanjay said to Zorgbon. "Come with me."

Zorgbon groaned, but Sanjay took his wrist and together they trotted out of the crowd and joined the young Vespian.

“Hello,” the Vespian said. “Great parade, isn’t it?”

“It’s fantastic,” Sanjay said. “But do you know the quickest way to the school sports ground?”

“Sure,” the Vespian said.

“We need to get there in a hurry,” Sanjay said.
“My friend is a star high jumper and he’ll miss out on the competition if we can’t get there in time.”

The Vespian looked at Zorgbon.
“You look like a star high jumper to me,” the Vespian said.
“Climb on board. I’ll get you there.”

Chapter 4

A Ride on a Vespian

Sanjay and Zorgbon climbed onto the Vespian's broad back. They held onto his neck horns.

"Here we go!" the Vespian said.

Soon they were galloping down the street while the Vespian blew multi-coloured bubbles from his snout.
"Whee!" the Vespian cried as they charged right through the middle of the parade. "This is fun!"

Sanjay and Zorgbon held on tightly as the mighty Vespian went faster and faster.

“Coming through!” the Vespian cried as the older Vespians scattered.

“Emergency!” he shouted, and the Snerdians leapfrogged out of the way.

“Special sports ground express!” he called, and the Hoffians nearly dropped their juggling clubs, plates and balls.

Sanjay grinned. This was the best! “Hey, Zorgbon,” he said. “Wave to the other Fleenbeens as we go past!”

Zorgbon groaned. “I feel sick.”

Soon, they reached the sports ground.
The Vespian stopped right outside the entrance.
"Here we are!" he said.

Zorgbon groaned. "Thank goodness," he said as he slid off the Vespian's back.

"Are we in time?" the Vespian asked.

"Yes," Sanjay said. "How can we thank you?"

"Win the high-jump competition for me," the Vespian said.
He nudged Zorgbon with his beak. "Set a new record."

Ms Edo hurried through the gate.
"Quick, Zorgbon! Your event is just about to start!"

Chapter 5

A New School Record

"Now, remember," Sanjay said to Zorgbon. "Ten steps, push off with your left foot, arch your back, twist, flip your legs, and kick."

Zorgbon looked at the other competitors. "They look very good. Maybe I should just give up now," he said.

Sanjay patted his friend on the shoulder. "If you do your best, you'll be a winner, no matter what happens."

"Really?" asked Zorgbon.

"Truly," replied Sanjay.

Zorgbon only had to jump once. None of the other competitors even came close to beating him.

“Zorgbon has set a new school record!” Ms Edo announced, after she’d spoken with the judges.

Everyone cheered.

Zorgbon smiled. He held up his winner's ribbon.
"It's a nice colour," he said to Sanjay.

"It suits you," Sanjay said.
"Now, how about training for the long jump next year?"